BE AN ECO HERO!

ON THE MOVE

Florence Urquhart and Lisa Koesterke

W

FRANKLIN WATTS

LONDON • SYDNEY

BE AN ECO HERO!

We hope you enjoy this book.
Please return or renew it by the due date.
You can renew it at **www.norfolk.gov.uk/libraries**
or by using our free library app. Otherwise you can
phone **0344 800 8020** - please have your library
card and pin ready.
You can sign up for email reminders too.

ON THE MOVE

Franklin Watts
First published in Great Britain in 2022 by The Watts Publishing Group

Credits
Design and project management: Raspberry Books
Art Direction & cover design: Sidonie Beresford-Browne
Designer: Vanessa Mee
Illustrations: Lisa Koesterke

HB ISBN: 978 1 4451 8183 7
PB ISBN: 978 1 4451 8184 4

Printed in China

MIX
Paper from
responsible sources
FSC® C104740
FSC
www.fsc.org

Franklin Watts
An imprint of
Hachette Children's Group
Part of The Watts Publishing Group
Carmelite House
50 Victoria Embankment
London EC4Y 0DZ

An Hachette UK Company
www.hachette.co.uk

www.hachettechildrens.co.uk

CONTENTS

ON THE MOVE

Every day, all over the world,
we move around in different ways.
We walk or ride a bike, but we also
travel in vehicles, such as cars,
buses, trains and planes.

We also use lorries, vans and planes.
They carry things that we need, such as
clothes, toys and food from place to place.

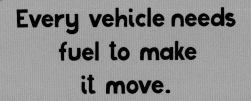

Every vehicle needs fuel to make it move.

How do you travel around?

7

FOSSIL FUELS

Most vehicles run on petrol or diesel. These are made from a fossil fuel called oil. Fossil fuels are made from plant and animal materials.

Fossil fuels take millions and millions of years to form under the ground.

We are using up fossil fuels very quickly. Once we run out of fossil fuels it will take millions of years for more to form.

An oil rig is used to drill down deep below the sea to find oil.

Fuel is very important to us. Eco heroes don't waste it!

USING LESS
FUEL

There are lots of simple things you and your family can do to save fuel.

BE AN ECO HERO BY:

Helping to empty the car boot.

If a car boot is full the car is much heavier. The car has to use more fuel if the car is heavy.

Opening the window instead of asking to use the air conditioning. It takes fuel to use the air conditioning.

Helping to take off roof racks and top boxes when you do not need them. A roof rack or top box slows the car down and uses more fuel.

Reminding adults to check tyre pressures. Having tyres at the right pressure saves fuel.

You can be an eco hero by using less energy. For example, you can help to choose light bulbs that are energy efficient. This means they use less energy and last much longer.

AIR POLLUTION

Most vehicles on the road cause pollution. As their engines use fuel they make gases that can poison the air and cause global warming.

Ships, planes and some trains also pump out gases that are very bad for the planet.

We breathe in these gases and it can be bad for us. Pollution in the air also mixes with rain. This makes acid rain, which can damage trees and buildings.

These trees have been killed by acid rain.

Take fewer journeys by car and plane and reduce pollution!

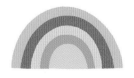

SHORT JOURNEYS

BE AN ECO HERO BY ...

... cutting down on car use.

For a short journey, such as going to school, try not to travel by car. See if you can find another way to travel and you will:

SAVE FUEL

HELP TO CLEAN THE AIR

REDUCE POLLUTION

go by scooter

walk or run

use a skateboard

CAR SHARE

Many people use their cars to travel
to work and to school.

If you make everyday
journeys like this, you
could work out a
car share rota.

Be an eco hero by
giving someone a ride or
getting one yourself.

If you share a car journey, the car is full
rather than carrying just one or two people.
This means fewer cars on the road, which
causes less pollution. The roads are safer too.

RIDING A BIKE

You can be an ECO HERO
by riding a bike.

This is good for the planet and
it is also good for you.

RIDING A BIKE ...

... does not use petrol, does not cause pollution and keeps you fit!

Remember to cycle safely!

Wear a helmet and make sure your bike has a bell and lights on the front and back.

bell

helmet

light

TRAVEL BY BUS

You are an ECO HERO if you travel by bus or tram. This is a good way to use less fuel and cut down on pollution.

Travelling by bus or tram means less traffic on the roads. A 30-seater bus can mean 30 fewer cars on the road.

If you go on a day trip, try to find out if you can travel by bus.

Travelling on a bus with your friends is fun.

TRAVEL BY TRAIN

Trains are a fast way to travel around. Train travel can help save fuel, reduce traffic and cut down on pollution.

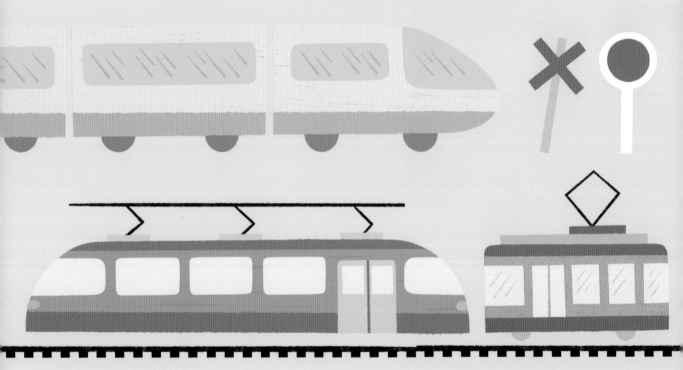

It can also be more fun to travel by train.

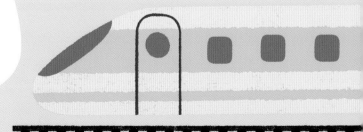

Travelling on a full train is better than each person travelling in their own car.

It cuts down on traffic jams too.

ECO SHOPPING

Every day, lorries, vans, planes and trains transport food all over the planet. This makes more traffic, uses fuel and causes pollution.

BE AN ECO HERO BY:

Reading food labels to find out how far your food has travelled and choosing local food if you can. The food will be fresher and you will be helping local farmers.

Walk or cycle to your local shops if you can.

When you buy online, save up your shopping so things can be delivered together.

only buy what
you really need

choose
local food

A van delivering
to 50 homes means
50 fewer cars on
the road.

home
delivery

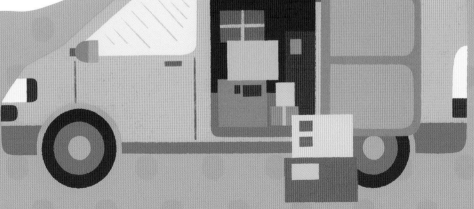

ECO HERO ACTIVITIES

Here are some eco hero activities
you could do at home.

HELP YOUR FRIENDS TO BE ECO HEROES!

Make a poster to show all the ways to
get around without causing pollution.

You could use
pictures from
magazines or
the Internet.

BE AN ECO HERO!
DON'T TRAVEL BY CAR.

WALK, CYCLE OR
GO BY SCOOTER OR
SKATEBOARD INSTEAD!

Ask an adult to help you write a letter to your council asking for more cycle paths where you live.

Learn how your bike works and how to clean and mend it.

Clean bikes last for longer.

Bicycle lanes make cycling safer.

QUIZ

1. Why is it important to use less fossil fuels?

a. They need lots of rest
b. It will take millions of years for more to form
c. They are too messy

2. What is the fossil fuel used to make petrol and diesel?

a. Oil
b. Sugar
c. Coal

3. Which of these changes could help to save fuel?

a. Put something heavy into the car boot
b. Open the window instead of using air conditioning
c. Drive everywhere you go

4. What is pollution?

a. The sound of birds singing
b. A vehicle that runs along a track
c. Gas or liquid that dirties or poisons air or water

5. How can you save fuel when going on a short journey?

a. Fly in a plane
b. Walk, cycle, or go by scooter
c. Drive in the car

6. Why is riding a bike good for the planet?

a. It is fun
b. It keeps you fit
c. It does not use petrol or cause pollution

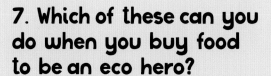

7. Which of these can you do when you buy food to be an eco hero?

a. Look for locally grown food
b. Drive to the shop
c. Buy food that was made far away

8. Which of these is a good way to reduce the number of cars on the road?

a. Everyone driving to work
b. Taking a bus, train or tram to work
c. Playing music in the car

9. What should you always wear when you ride your bike or scooter?

a. Yellow socks
b. A helmet
c. Shorts

10. What will you do to be an eco hero today?

ANSWERS:

1) b. It will take millions of years for more to form
2) a. Oil
3) b. Open the window instead of using air conditioning
4) c. Gas or liquid that dirties or poisons air or water
5) b. Walk, cycle, or go by scooter
6) c. It does not use petrol or cause pollution
7) a. Look for locally grown food
8) b. Taking a bus, train or tram to work
9) b. A helmet

What did you score?

1-3:
It would be a good idea to read the book again.

4-6:
You're almost there.

7-10:
You are an eco hero!

GLOSSARY

acid rain rain that is full of dangerous chemicals.

diesel a type of fuel made from oil.

fossil fuel materials found deep under the ground and formed over millions of years from dead animals and plants.

fuel material used to make heat or light, usually by being burned. Coal, gas and oil are types of fuel.

gas air-like substance that you cannot see.

global warming worldwide rise in temperatures affecting sea levels and weather.

local a person, place or shop that is in your neighbourhood.

oil thick, dark liquid found deep under the ground.

oil rig a structure used for drilling for oil.

petrol a type of fuel made from oil.

pollution gas or liquid that dirties or poisons air or water.

rota a list of dates and times and who does what.

tram a vehicle that runs along a fixed track.

transport to move people or things from place to place.

LEARN MORE

This book shows you some of the ways you can be an eco hero when you're on the move. But there is plenty more you can do to save the planet. Here are some websites that have lots of ideas and information to help you learn more about being an eco hero:

https://ecofriendlykids.co.uk
The Travelling section of the website includes advice on reducing unnecessary travel and making the school run more eco-friendly.

https://www.natgeokids.com/uk/discover/science/nature/how-to-save-the-planet/
Tips on how to save the planet from National Geographic Kids, including when you're on the move.

For parents and teachers

https://friendsoftheearth.uk/climate-change/responsible-travel
Plenty of eco-friendly travel ideas, from walking and cycling more to switching to an electric car.

www.wwf.org.uk/get-involved/schools/resources
This site offers curriculum linked resources for teachers to help children explore a variety of environmental themes.

Note to parents and teachers: Every effort has been made by the Publishers to ensure that these websites are suitable for children, that they are of the highest educational value, and that they contain no inappropriate or offensive material. However, because of the nature of the Internet, it is impossible to guarantee that the contents of these sites will not be altered. We strongly advise that Internet access is supervised by a responsible adult.

INDEX